Bantam Books in the Choose Your Own Adventure® Series
Ask your bookseller for the books you have missed

VOLCANO!

BY MERYL SIEGMAN

ILLUSTRATED BY TED ENIK

An R.A. Montgomery Book

BANTAM BOOKS
TORONTO · NEW YORK · LONDON · SYDNEY · AUCKLAND

RL 4, IL age 10 and up

VOLCANO
A Bantam Book / January 1987

CHOOSE YOUR OWN ADVENTURE® is a registered trademark of
Bantam Books, Inc. Registered in U.S. Patent and Trademark
Office and elsewhere.
Original conception of Edward Packard.

ISBN 0-553-26197-5

Published simultaneously in the United States and Canada

PRINTED IN THE UNITED STATES OF AMERICA

O   0 9 8 7 6 5 4

VOLCANO!

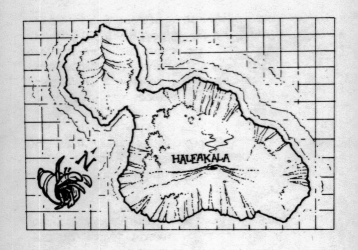

WARNING!!!

Do not read this book straight through from beginning to end. These pages contain many different adventures you may have as you explore Haleakala, a Hawaiian volcano. From time to time as you read along, you will be asked to make decisions and choices. Your choices may lead to success or disaster.

Your adventures are the result of your choices. You are responsible because you choose! After you make your choice, follow the instructions to see what happens next.

Think carefully before you make a move. Beware as you search for a silver sword hidden in the volcano; Haleakala could erupt at any time!

Good luck!

Author's Note

Haleakala (pronounced hah'-lay-ah-kah-lah') is a Hawaiian word that translates roughly as "The House of the Sun." In Hawaii, there is a mountain named Haleakala because long ago, according to legend, the demigod Maui imprisoned the sun's rays there and made him promise to lengthen the hours of daylight on the mountain.

"Aloha!" calls Jon, your next-door neighbor and best friend, as he rides into your corral. "What's up?"

"I'm grooming Makena so I can ride her into the crater tomorrow when I go camping," you reply.

"Again?" cries your friend in disbelief. "This'll be the sixth weekend in a row you've gone searching for the Silver Sword. When will you give up?"

"Not until I find it," you say with a smile, continuing to comb Makena's tail.

You live on the Hawaiian island of Maui. Your parents are ranchers like everyone else on this side of the island. Your small town rests at the foot of Haleakala, a volcanic mountain that rises ten thousand feet above sea level. At the top of the mountain lies an enormous crater filled with cinder cones, lava flows, and minicraters. It's so large that it has areas of desert and forest. There's even a lake in the crater!

Turn to page 2.

2

Six weeks ago in Hawaiian history class you learned about an ancient silver sword that is said to be lost or hidden somewhere in the crater. It belonged to King Ola, Maui's first ruler. According to legend, it has the power to stop a volcanic eruption. That night after class you dreamed that you found the sword. Ever since, you've been determined to be the first one to find it.

"I heard on the news tonight that Haleakala is beginning to swell," Jon tells you. "It could erupt any time."

"They've been saying that for weeks," you remind your friend. "Besides, Haleakala hasn't erupted in over two hundred years. Those scientists' reports don't scare me."

Jon still doesn't look sure.

"Why don't you come?" you say mischievously. "I could use your help."

"Sure," Jon replies much to your surprise. "I'll come."

"Great. Meet me here tomorrow morning at sunup," you tell him.

Turn to page 8.

Leading the horses by their reins, you bushwack through the jungle, cutting away limbs and vines, until you pick up the trail again.

"Now the trick is to make it to the top of the mountain as quickly as possible so we can start looking for the Silver Sword," you tell Jon as you set off.

Soon the trail no longer cuts through the jungle, but through open fields. You push your horses onward. The midmorning sun bears down and bakes your skin.

Turn to page 9.

You cross the dam and ride toward the rim of the crater. As you climb, you leave the jungle behind. Soon an enormous, dense bamboo forest looms in front of you.

"That stuff sure is tall," Jon exclaims. "Some of those stalks must be a hundred feet high."

Your trail branches into two paths. One leads around the forest. Another cuts into thick bamboo growth and then disappears in the darkness.

"You're not thinking about going in there, are you?" Jon asks cautiously, peering inside. "Horses can't see very well in the dark."

"I know a shortcut through the bamboo forest that will cut out miles of steep climbing and save the horses' energy too. But," you add with a frown, "the forest *does* look awfully dark."

If you decide to enter the bamboo forest, turn to page 21.

If you decide to go around the forest instead, turn to page 47.

"I know this place really well," you reassure your friend. "If we go just a little farther, we'll come to a bend. Maybe from there we can see light. Just go slowly."

You crawl on inch by inch. It seems as if it takes forever to go even a few feet.

"Ouch!" Jon yells. "I just bumped my head. Get me out of here, quick."

"Wait!" you exclaim. "What's that?" You see a dim light in the distance. It seems to be coming from a crack between two rocks. You move toward it as quickly as possible. The closer you get, the brighter the light glows.

"Something's under this pile of rocks," Jon says excitedly. Rapidly you begin removing the stones. When you're done, you can hardly believe your eyes. Lying at your feet is a shining silver sword! Its light illuminates the Lava Tube for at least twenty feet.

Turn to page 31.

The next day Jon arrives on his horse Hana, just as the sun rises over the lip of the ocean. Your saddlebags are filled with food and water, extra clothing, and camping gear. Everything is ready. You ride out of the barn, and you and Jon point the horses toward the trail. You've only traveled a hundred yards when the ground begins to shake and you hear a low rumbling.

"What's that?" cries Jon.

You look up at Haleakala. Its highest peaks rise above a layer of clouds. Smoke is pouring out of the top of the volcano.

"I don't know about this camping trip," Jon says, his voice unsteady.

"Oh, that's been going on for days. If it looks bad when we get up there, we'll turn back," you assure him. "Look, the smoke has already stopped."

Jon nods and you continue on your way. The sun is rising over the Pacific, and its warm reflection feels like a good omen.

Turn to page 10.

Late in the morning, you reach the rim of Haleakala and peer into the enormous crater. It's more than two thousand feet deep. Several trails descend from the rim, crisscross the crater floor, and then rise to the distant peaks. Hikers use these trails often.

"Which way are we going now?" Jon asks.

"Last week I received photocopies of two articles on Hawaiian legends," you confide. "They came from a special library in San Francisco. I'd been waiting for them for weeks. One article says that King Ola hid the Silver Sword in the Bottomless Pit. He thought that the enemy tribes who sought the sword would never look there."

"What does the other article say?" Jon asks.

"Well," you say slowly, "it's a more recent article that claims the sword is buried in the Lava Tube."

Jon looks confused. "Where should we go—the Bottomless Pit or the Lava Tube?"

If you decide to head for the Bottomless Pit, turn to page 103.

If you decide to search the Lava Tube first, turn to page 14.

The trail from your ranch leads into a jungle thick with huge ferns and hanging vines. The air is damp and heavy. You start to climb the mountain slowly. You have a long day ahead, and you don't want to tire your horses.

Suddenly the trail comes to a river and bends to the right.

"Gee, the river looks low this year," Jon comments. "I bet we could cross it with the horses."

"You're right," you say, pulling Makena to a stop. "It would save us almost a mile too. The bridge is still a long way off."

"On the other hand, we might get our saddlebags wet. There's nothing worse than a waterlogged peanut butter sandwich!" Jon replies. "What do you think we should do?"

If you decide to try to cross the river with the horses, turn to page 36.

If you decide to continue to the bridge, turn to page 13.

In another few hours the helicopter is hovering not far overhead. The co-pilot descends on a rope ladder. "We've got some special harnesses to hitch to the horses," he says when he alights. "We'll tranquilize them, and then take them out one at a time.

Jon and Hana go first. You wait with Makena as Hana is fastened to the helicopter with a contraption made of chains and netting. Jon scrambles into the helicopter, which starts to rise, gently lifting Hana off the ground.

Shortly after, the pilot returns for you and Makena. As you're lifted out of the crater, you feel relieved that you're safe from a possible eruption. But you know you will never feel completely content as long as the Silver Sword remains hidden somewhere inside the House of the Sun.

The End

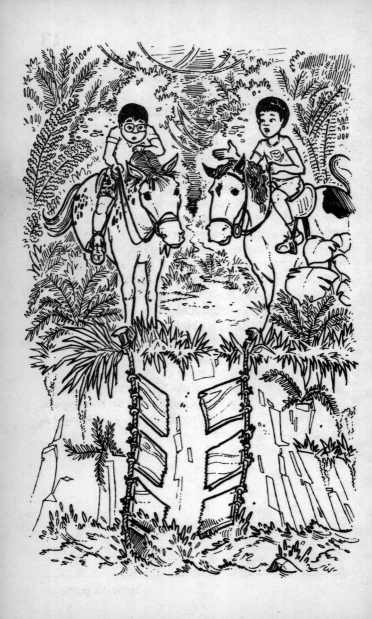

"Crossing here will be hard on the horses. One of them could slip," you say.

Jon nods and you continue upstream along the trail.

"Oh, no!" Jon cries when you arrive at the bridge. The wooden planks in the middle have been sawed in half. It's impossible to cross. "Why would anyone do a thing like this?" Jon asks.

"I don't want to scare you, but I've read in the paper that the police suspect smugglers are stashing goods somewhere on the mountain. Someone may be trying to protect a hiding spot. Of course," you add quickly when you see a worried expression flicker across Jon's face, "vandals or even the Menehunes could have wrecked the bridge." The Menehunes are a mythical tribe of little people who are said to inhabit Haleakala.

You know of only one other way across the river at a dam farther up the trail. It will take you out of your way, but you have no choice.

"We'll have to trot awhile to make up for lost time," you tell Jon as you explain the route you have chosen. "But we should arrive at the top of Haleakala before noon."

Turn to page 5.

The trail to the Lava Tube is incredibly hot and dry. Lava from past eruptions has hardened into eerie shapes all around you. The landscape is just what you've imagined the moon looks like. Nothing is growing—except your thirst. You take a small sip of precious water from your canteen.

"Hey, look!" Jon shouts.

Ahead of you is a field of shiny objects, but they're just plants called silverswords, or *ahinahina* in Hawaiian. They were named after King Ola's sword because of their shiny spikes. Silverswords don't grow anywhere in the world except in the craters of Hawaii.

"Those are plants," you tell Jon impatiently.

"No, I see a real sword, I swear it!" Jon cries. He spurs his horse and takes off through the field.

"Wait!" you yell after him, but it is too late. The sun's going to his head, you mutter to yourself. "Take it easy on your horse!" you shout, walking Makena slowly toward the crazy-looking plants.

Jon and Hana are waiting for you at the other end of the field, panting and soaked with sweat.

"I guess it was just a mirage," Jon admits sheepishly.

Turn to page 44.

"Some archaeologist!" Jon says with a snort. You peer into the Bottomless Pit. About seven or eight feet down, the pit turns sharply. Beyond that you see nothing.

"I'm going in," you announce. You take the rope that's tied to Makena's saddle and drop it into the pit. Then you stick your flashlight under your belt and start to lower yourself in. "Stand by Makena's head," you say to Jon, "and make sure she doesn't move. Here goes."

The passageway widens after the bend, and you find yourself suspended in a dark chamber. You realize with dismay that your rope isn't quite long enough to reach the bottom—it stops about ten feet short. You stand on the ledge Dudley landed on. Disappointed, you start to climb back up. Then the beam from your flashlight illuminates a bright object that is partly buried in the sandy ground.

"What do you see down there?" Jon shouts.

"Something shiny in the sand," you reply. "But I can't tell what it is and the rope's not long enough to reach the bottom."

If you decide to climb back up and go for more rope, turn to page 22.

If you want to jump down now, turn to page 46.

You squint, trying to get a better look at the shadowy figure. You wonder silently if it's Maui—the Polynesian demigod whose spirit, according to some, still inhabits the crater. Legend has it he once lassoed the sun's rays and tied them to a tree. This forced the sun to slow its journey across the sky so that the days in Haleakala would always be long. Your island is named after him.

You start to call Maui's name but stop. Jon will think you're crazy. Instead, you wave at the man, and he slowly turns and looks at you. You smile at him. You're not sure, but you think that he winked and, for a split second, smiled back. He continues to twirl his lasso. You stand for a moment in awe. You notice that smoke is no longer pouring out of the volcano.

"Let's keep going," Jon says.

Turn to page 99.

After a moment, the fiery current slows. In a few minutes it has stopped entirely.

The town has been saved, but not the Silver Sword. The molten lava has melted it. All that remains is part of its hilt, frozen forever in the solidified lava flow.

Your town is saved! Scientists the world over are stupefied by the sudden stop of Haleakala's eruption. When the hilt of King Ola's sword is discovered in the solidified lava flow by hikers a few years later, that becomes the popular explanation. Your role in the affair, however, always remains a secret.

The End

As you race back up the trail to the rim, the crater floor starts to tremble and shake. You're glad you took your brother's advice. You can feel Makena's heart pounding as she gallops through the sand and hardened lava. Jon and Hana are not far behind.

At the top of Haleakala while the horses catch their breath, you peer down into the crater, thinking sadly of the Silver Sword you'll never find. But a violent tremor makes you forget everything except getting out of the crater as quickly as possible. You and Jon race headlong down the mountain.

Turn to page 23.

It's as dark as night inside the bamboo forest, and your horses rely on you to guide them. As you slowly push your way through the bamboo stalks, they knock against each other, making a strange clacking sound. It's like being inside a giant musical instrument!

All at once you halt so suddenly that Jon and Hana crash into you. "Shhhh!" you warn. "Listen!"

You hear faint mumblings, like voices, in the distance.

"Let's check it out," you whisper.

Turn to page 61.

"If I jump, I could get stuck down here," you call. "I'm coming up. Hold on to Makena." You start the climb. Soon you're back on solid ground at the rim of the Bottomless Pit.

"We've got to think of a way to find out if that was the Silver Sword," you tell Jon. "My flashlight isn't very strong, but what I saw might have been the handle. I couldn't tell for sure."

"How much more rope do you need?"

"About another six feet," you answer. You and Jon stand around racking your brains for a solution. Unexpectedly, an enormous roar echoes through the crater.

"What was that?" shrieks Jon.

"Haleakala! Look!" High above you, the mountaintop is belching steam and ash.

"Quick!" you cry. "Get on Hana."

"What about the Silver Sword?"

"No time now. We'll look for it next time." But you know, looking up at the simmering mountaintop, there won't be a next time.

The End

Below, the town is in a state of chaos. The road to the airport is clogged with traffic, and some of the townspeople are rushing to the harbor in hopes of escaping by boat. Other villagers are heading on foot for high ground.

You ride through the village to your ranch just outside of town. Jon leaves you at the road to his house. When you get home, you see that the car is gone and the house is deserted. Just then, thick black smoke pours out of the crater and the ground shakes so hard you almost fall off your horse. Makena whinnies nervously and paws the ground.

Since your dad owns a small plane your folks are probably at the airport. But you may not have enough time to make it out there. The harbor is much closer, perhaps you should head for the water.

If you decide to go the airport and try to catch up with your parents, turn to page 67.

If you decide to go to the harbor and try to escape by boat, turn to page 26.

Once you hold the sword, Boris freezes in terror.

"We did it, Jon," you cry. "We've got the Silver Sword!"

"What's going on up there?" someone shouts from inside the cinder cone. "Get us out of here! Hey, Boris!"

"And we also caught some pretty serious criminals," Jon adds, smiling. "The police will be glad to see these guys—and all that counterfeit money."

"I'll stay here and guard Fatso," you say. "You go get help."

Jon gallops off on Hana. You sit in the shade holding the Silver Sword, never taking your eyes off Boris.

The End

26

You race back to town toward the harbor. As you pass the road to Jon's ranch, Hana and Jon gallop toward you.

"My house is deserted!" Jon shouts. "My parents must have gone to the harbor to get on their boat. Let's go!"

"That's where I was heading," you tell him excitedly, and together you canter to the shore. Near the harbor you leave your horses and fight your way through the crowd to where Jon's parents dock their fishing boat.

"I can't believe it! Our boat's gone!" Jon exclaims in disbelief.

Turn to page 42.

"Quick!" you order. "Help me unfasten the ladder!" You and Jon try to pry loose the steel pegs which secure the ladder, but they hold fast. The heavy man is already climbing up the ladder and his weight makes the job impossible.

"I can't pull these out" cries Jon desperately.

"Neither can I. Run!" Just as Boris's head emerges from the cinder cone, you and Jon flee down the steep slope.

Not so fast!" Boris's gruff voice bellows, but you keep on running.

"Freeze or I'll shoot!"

You stop. The thief is standing on the rim, pointing a gun at you. Soon he is joined by his friends. "Look what we have here," Boris says. "A couple of punks. What do you think we should do with them?"

Turn to page 49.

You forget all about your brother's warning as soon as you reach the entrance to the Lava Tube. Leaping from your horse, you stare down at a gaping black hole in the ground. "The Lava Tube," you announce.

"I know," Jon replies. "I've seen it before, but I've never gone in. You've actually been inside?"

"Sure," you answer. "Lots of times."

"How far does it go?"

"About half a mile, all underground. There's a place to climb out on the other side."

"Boy, it's dark in there!" Jon says, peering dubiously into the black entrance.

Go on to the next page.

"I brought a flashlight. Come on, let's get going. There's no time to lose. We've *got* to find the sword."

You tie your horses to a tree trunk in the shade and lower yourselves into the Tube.

Turn to page 90.

"Now what?" Jon asks.

"Now we wait," you reply testily.

You roll out your sleeping bags on the bumpy, uneven ground and spend the night trying unsuccessfully to get some rest.

At dawn, when you have finally drifted off into a light sleep, the whirring of a helicopter wakes you.

"What . . ." Jon mumbles.

"Why didn't I think of that before?" you exclaim. "The helicopters are out looking for hikers because of the volcano alert." You jump up and start waving your arms wildly. It's not long before the helicopter spots you. The pilot drops closer and signals that he is going to get help. You point to Makena and Hana, who are standing patiently nearby, probably wishing there was some grass to eat.

Turn to page 11.

You carry the sword ahead of you. It lights your way like a flashlight. In a short while you emerge from the tunnel. It's so bright outside you have to shield your eyes with your hand. As you remove your hand, you realize that the strong glare comes partly from King Ola's sword which gleams brilliantly in the sun.

With great excitement you hike back to where you left Makena and Hana. The horses are fresh and ready to go after their rest. You take off toward the high mountains. As you climb you notice that what started as a slight vibration when you emerged from the Tube, is now a constant tremble. And it's rapidly growing more violent.

Suddenly a dark shadow covers the sun. You look up. A thick cloud of ash is spewing out of the top of the crater. Then, like fireworks, pieces of burning lava shoot off in all directions, making fizzing, crackling noises. You don't have time to watch the rest of the fiery display. "Let's get up to the top," you yell to Jon. "Before Haleakala blows and we're stuck down here for good!"

You drive your horses up the steep path. As you reach the top of the crater, a violent explosion of steam, ash, and rock bursts from the crater. A liquid fire starts to tumble down the mountainside toward the town. You know it won't be long before the lava reaches your ranch.

Turn to page 89.

Shortly after Jon leaves, the ground begins to rumble. Sand pours in on you through the opening thirty feet above. Hurry, Jon, you think nervously. The minutes tick by. Each one seems like an hour. "What's taking him so long?" you say impatiently.

A hissing sound interrupts your thoughts. "What's that?" you shout, jumping to your feet. You point your flashlight toward the noise and see a snake poised not more than four feet in front of you. You freeze, afraid to move a single muscle.

Hurry, Jon, hurry, is your last thought before the snake strikes.

The End

"We don't have time to collect the rocks," you say to your friend, "We have to explore the Bubble Cave before dark."

You continue your descent into the crater. Jon looks back wistfully at the hardened lava but follows you. The trip along the trail is slow, uneventful, and hot.

"I know this sounds silly, but I'm not sure what the Bubble Cave *is*," Jon says after awhile.

"It's a cave formed by an air pocket in the lava flow many years ago," you explain. "Even though the ancient Hawaiians never actually lived in the crater, they often spent a night or two inside, since it was so sacred. And they used the Bubble Cave for shelter. Maybe someone hid the Silver Sword there. Even if we don't find it, we can camp there and start looking again early tomorrow morning."

Turn to page 107.

You and John grope through the darkness. Sharp rocks and huge boulders threaten you at every turn. It's impossible to hurry. You inch along for what seems like hours. You don't hear one peep out of Jon.

Finally, you see light shining through an opening in the rocks. You've made it out of the Lava Tube.

Makena and Hana are trembling and pulling at their tethers. All around you the ground is shaking violently. There's no time to lose. You and Jon mount your horses and race toward the rim of the crater. There's no need to push your horses; sensing danger, they gallop as fast as they can. A low rumble fills the crater and grows louder as you canter on.

Turn to page 53.

You lead Makena down the steep embankment to the river's edge and spur her on. She seems shocked that you are asking her to cross the river, but she trusts you and responds to your command. Jon is right behind you on Hana.

The horses step into the water and tread along carefully, slipping occasionally on the rocky bed. By the time you reach the middle of the river, the rushing water is up to the horses' bellies.

"Oh no!" you cry out. "The saddlebags!"

From above, the river looked more shallow than it actually is. But now water is rising over the seams of the bags, wetting at least some of your gear.

"I hope none of the food's ruined," Jon shouts.

Finally, you reach the far bank. "The horses aren't too happy," you say, "but at least the water will cool them off for a while." You reward each animal with a piece of papaya before traveling on.

Turn to page 4.

"Mr. Crake," you say to the archaeologist.

"*Dr.* Crake," he corrects you. "But call me Dudley."

"Do you know where to find the Silver Sword?"

"According to my instruments, the Crake Sword . . . I mean, King Ola's sword, lies two point one miles northeast of here, in a place called the Bottomless Pit."

"I think it may be in the Bottomless Pit too!" you exclaim excitedly. "I've been looking for the sword myself."

"Then we can search together," the archaeologist offers generously.

You and Jon introduce yourselves to Dudley, and the three of you start down the trail again.

You're tempted to charge off on Makena in order to reach the pit more quickly, but Dudley's pack is too loaded down. He walks at a snail's pace, equipment clinking and clanking with every step. Finally, you come to the sign indicating the rim of the Bottomless Pit. The archaeologist has jogged the last few hundred feet, and is panting when he arrives.

"This, my friends," he says grandly, "may be the culmination of a lifetime of work. I need only the elusive sword to complete the Crake Collection."

Turn to page 86.

You pull Makena's rein sharply and veer off the trail. Here the shrubbery is so thick that it's practically impossible to ride through it, but at least you're safer than on the trail. After half a minute, the thundering landslide slows and then stops. You wait for the sand and dust to settle.

"If we're going to go anywhere," you tell Jon, "we'll have to get back on the trail. We can't ride through this brush; it's too dense."

"But the trail looks blocked," he replies. "We can't make it. We'll have to wait for help."

"Wait for help?" you echo, looking up at the smoking mountaintop.

"I don't see how we can get the horses through that rubble," Jon answers.

You scout the trail yourself. It will be dangerous, if not impossible, to pass. But if you wait, who knows how long it will take to be rescued. Eventually you may have to try to get out on your own anyway.

If you decide to stay where you are and wait for help, turn to page 92.

If you decide to try to get back on the trail, turn to page 83.

"Can you hear me?" you call into the pit. "I'm coming after you."

"Of course I can hear you," Dudley yells back. "I'm on a ledge of some kind. Hurry up and get me out of here!"

"Are you hurt?"

"No, I'm not hurt. Just get me out of here before I get bitten by a snake."

You grab the rope that's tied to your saddle and lead Makena to the edge of the pit. You check to make sure the saddle is tightly cinched. Then you throw the rope into the pit.

"Help!" you hear. "A snake!"

"No, it's a rope. Grab hold and come on up," you order.

The rope is pulled taut as the archaeologist starts his climb. At the other end Makena strains hard. At last, Dudley emerges, panting and exhausted. "What did you see down there?" you ask eagerly.

He looks into the pit and shudders. "I honestly didn't notice. I was concentrating on nothing but my immediate departure from that wretched place." He hoists his pack onto his back and walks off, equipment clattering.

"Hey, what about the Silver Sword?" you call after him.

Dudley stops for a moment. "Anyone who wants to subject himself to that . . . that disgusting place can have it," he states and continues on his way.

Turn to page 15.

The red-faced man's angry expression softens a bit.

The police officer looks at you kindly. "Why don't you kids head on home? We've had enough excitement for one day."

The owner of the boat decides not to press charges.

On the way home, Jon tries to cheer you up, saying, "Well, at least you didn't get arrested."

"Some consolation," you reply. "That thief and his loot are probably halfway to Pago Pago by now."

"I have a great idea. Let's go surfing," Jon suggests.

"Yeah, why not?" you agree. "I think I need a break from this whole Silver Sword thing for a while."

The End

All around you people are crowding onto boats. You spot the *Hand Maiden,* the large cruise ship that docks regularly at Maui. "I'll bet there's room for us," you say, and push your way toward it. You recognize a friend of your father's. "Come on, kids," he urges. "We have room for two more." You and Jon jump on board. The man tosses you life jackets. "Just in time," he says. "These are our last two."

Within minutes the *Hand Maiden* heaves out of the harbor. You watch the island grow smaller as you head out to sea. Then, suddenly, it happens. You hear a thundering roar. The whole island seems to be on fire. Flames and pieces of rock shoot out of the top of Haleakala and rumble down the side of the mountain. It feels as if the *Hand Maiden* is being lifted out of the water, and then you realize that a giant tidal wave is about to capsize the boat.

"Quick, jump!" you hear someone shout. You have no choice. You take a deep breath and plunge into the sea.

The End

As you continue on toward the Lava Tube you hear a funny sound. "Beep-beep! Beep-beep!"

"What's that?" Jon asks.

"I'm not sure, but it sounds like my walkie-talkie. And it sounds like it's coming from my saddlebag." You dismount and search through your bag. In a moment you find one of the walkie-talkies you always bring along on camping trips. You're surprised it still works after your trip across the river. The walkie-talkie beeps again, and you push the answer button.

"Hello, I hear you, over," you shout into the receiver. You hear a lot of static and then recognize your younger brother's voice. He sounds excited.

"Am I ever glad I reached you! I just heard on the radio that Haleakala is going to . . ."

"What? I can hardly hear you. Speak louder!" you yell.

"You better get out of there fast. You don't have much time, only . . ." You can't make out the rest of the sentence through the static. Then you hear nothing at all.

Go on to the next page.

Jon stares at you, his eyes wide with fear. "Well, what are we waiting for?" he demands. "Come on!"

Despite your brother's warning the crater seems calm. And you're *so* close to the Lava Tube you'd hate to give up the search for King Ola's sword now.

If you think you'd better heed your brother's warning, turn to page 19.

If you hurry to the Lava Tube instead, turn to page 28.

Thinking of nothing but the Silver Sword, you let go of the rope and drop to the sandy floor, landing with a thud. You get up and grope your way over to the shiny object, grabbing hold of it expectantly. It feels rough. Inspecting it with your flashlight, you discover that it's only a cylindrical piece of lava rock. What you thought might have been jewels are merely air bubbles hardened in the lava.

"Did you find it?" Jon's voice echoes down to you.

"Yes, and it's not the Silver Sword. It's just a crummy piece of rock." You hear Jon laughing. "It's not funny," you yell up. "How am I going to get out of here? I can't reach the end of the rope."

"I'll get some more at the ranger station. I'll be quick," Jon calls, and then adds, "Don't go any-where."

"Very funny," you call. "Hurry!" You hear the clatter of hooves as Jon gallops off on Hana.

Turn to page 33.

The trail leading around the bamboo forest climbs steeply for several miles, past mountain pools and waterfalls. You'd like to go for a swim, but you know that the currents can be very dangerous. Besides, you don't have any time to spare.

Finally, just when you thought you'd never get there, you reach the rim of the crater. You are now ten thousand feet above sea level, so high that the clouds are far below you. A single misstep could mean a fall of a thousand feet or more. You feel as if you're standing on top of the world. The air is thin and you feel a bit dizzy.

The crater was once filled with liquid fire. Now you can see cinder cones, extinguished mini-craters, and lava flows. Hawaiian legend says that at one time, this was the home of Pele, the goddess of volcanoes. It is also a giant labyrinth that just might lead to the Silver Sword.

"Where to now?" John asks.

"Well, I had wanted to check the Bottomless Pit today, but it's too far off. From here it makes more sense to go to the Bubble Cave or a *heiau* I've heard about near here." A *heiau* is an ancient Hawaiian shrine that to an untrained eye looks like a pile of rocks. "The *heiau* will be harder to find, but there may be other campers visiting the Bubble Cave," you say. "It's a popular site."

If you decide to head toward the Bubble Cave, turn to page 52.

If you decide you would rather check out the heiau, turn to page 82.

"Grab them!" shouts one of the others.

You do not resist as the men seize you and gag you. "Bring them up here," Boris orders from the top of the cone. When you and Jon reach him, he commands, "Climb in." He keeps his gun pointed at the two of you as you descend the rope ladder. One of the men climbs down after you and binds your hands behind your backs. Then he climbs back out, pries the pegs from the ground, and rolls up the ladder.

"Have fun, kids," Boris calls down to you. "And stay out of trouble." He laughs cruelly. Soon the sound of the men's footsteps fades away.

Maybe, just maybe, you think, someone will find your horses and come looking for you.

The End

You tie the horses to a bamboo tree and tiptoe over to the side of the shack. The voices coming from inside are loud and clear.

"This volcano's about to blow, Boris. Let's clear the stuff out of the crater. It's not a safe hiding place anymore."

"Angelo is right, Boris. We should do it today. We don't have much time." This voice has a British accent.

Then you hear a gruff-sounding voice say, "But the *Molokai* is pulling out of the harbor this evening. She's a perfect target. I'd hate to pass up the opportunity."

"We have time to do both," the Englishman says. "We'll go into the crater and get the goods out of the big cinder cone. We can hide them, do the job after dark, and then head out. We could be in Pago Pago by daybreak."

"Okay," Boris replies, "but we gotta act fast."

You and Jon stare at each other for a moment. "These guys must be smugglers—not campers," you whisper. "And it sounds like Boris is their leader. We'd better get moving!"

Go on to the next page.

"What do you mean?" Jon asks.

"We're going to the cinder cone too. We've got to. They may even have the Silver Sword hidden there! On horseback we're faster than they are. We can get up there before they do and wait to see what they've stashed there."

"Wait a minute. That sounds dangerous," Jon protests. "Besides, they're probably armed. I say we head back to the harbor to warn the captain of the *Molokai*."

If you insist on riding to the cinder cone, turn to page 58.

If you decide to follow Jon's advice and go directly to warn the captain, turn to page 98.

"How do we get to the Bubble Cave?" Jon asks.

"We stay on this trail," you reply, pointing down to the road that zigzags down the wall of the crater.

You set off, the horses doing a slow walk. The beauty of Haleakala is tantalizing, but you become dizzy each time you look over the edge of the narrow trail.

Pieces of hard, black lava are everywhere, glittering in the sun. "The lava is amazing," Jon comments. "Each piece is unique. Look, that one looks like a racing car. Let's take some of these rocks home, coat them with shellac, and sell them as paperweights."

"I don't think that's a good idea," you warn. "What about the curse of Pele? Bad luck comes to anyone who removes rocks from Haleakala Crater."

"That's just superstition" scoffs Jon.

"Remember when Dan Ohana broke his leg last month? He told me that a week before the accident he'd gone camping in the crater and taken a couple of rocks. After he broke his leg, he got so scared he asked me to bring the rocks back to Haleakala on my next camping trip."

"But just think how much money we could make," Jon persists. "Come on, help me put a few into my saddlebag."

If you try to persuade your friend to leave the rocks alone, turn to page 34.

If you let Jon take the rocks, turn to page 73.

The rumbling becomes deafening as you near the crater's rim. You don't stop to rest at the top, but continue at full speed down the side of Haleakala. Once you glance over your shoulder and see thick clouds of smoke billowing out of the crater, showering the mountainside with ash and rocky debris.

Hana stumbles, sending Jon headlong into the shrubbery. "Are you hurt?" you ask. Jon gets up and brushes himself off. "I don't think so," he replies. But Hana is limping, and you notice that he has cut his knee badly on the sharp rocks.

Now you have to travel more slowly. You continue down the trail. All at once you hear an explosion and are blinded by a burst of smoke and fire that gushes out of the crater behind you.

Turn to page 70.

Jon hesitates.

"What if he has the Silver Sword?" you scream. This time Jon responds by starting to lower a foot into the boat.

"Just what do you think you're doing?" you hear over the purr of the engine. "That's my boat. Get away from there!" A red-faced man with a crewcut has come up behind Jon and grabbed him by the arm.

"Come on, Jon!" you shout. But you see that the man will not let go of your friend, who is looking at you helplessly.

"Get off my boat, thief," the man screams at you, his face getting even redder. You try to put the engine in reverse. "Okay, kid, you asked for it!" He lets go of Jon and jumps into the boat with you. He's a lot bigger and a lot stronger than you are. Before you know it, he has you in a chokehold. You're afraid he's going to try to strangle you, but when you stop struggling, he loosens his grasp.

Turn to page 69.

You quickly return to your horses and retrace your steps through the bamboo forest. "Never mind warning *them* about camping restrictions," you tell Jon. "I think *we* need to warn the *police.* They should know about these poachers as soon as possible."

"What about the Silver Sword?" Jon asks.

"Another time. We've got to stop that smuggling ring before all the nenes disappear forever."

You race down the mountain. At the bottom, you gallop along the road that leads to the nearest town. At the police station you breathlessly explain what you saw inside the bamboo forest.

"Well done," the sergeant tells you. "We've known about the operation for weeks but just couldn't discover where the poachers were hiding out. I'll arrange for a stakeout right away. It'll be all over for those guys."

Turn to page 74.

"Let's continue," you say, starting to pack the gear. "We can't let a silly dream stop us."

The early morning is cool. You and your horses feel refreshed as you head out to find the Bubble Cave.

The inside of the crater glows red and orange in the early morning sun. "This is my favorite time of day on Haleakala," you tell Jon.

"It's beautiful," he agrees.

You've already forgotten about your dream, and you think with excitement about having the whole day to search for the Silver Sword.

Turn to page 76.

"We'll be careful," you assure Jon as you point your horses in the direction of the cinder cone. "Remember, we can escape quickly on the horses if things get hairy."

At Haleakala's ten thousand-foot summit, the air is thin and chilly. You can see the horses' breath as they pant after the long climb.

You and Jon gaze down into Haleakala's enormous crater, dotted with cinder cones and small craters. "From way up here they look like anthills," Jon says. You follow the trail down to the crater bottom. The horses trot along the barren landscape to a group of cinder cones that are clustered together.

Go on to the next page.

"That's the one the men were talking about," you tell Jon, pointing to the tallest. "Let's hide behind a smaller cinder cone and wait for them. Those thieves won't be here for a couple of hours."

You lie down in the shade of your hideout and snooze. The horses wait patiently nearby. Later, the sound of voices awakens you. You peer out from your hiding place and see three men climbing to the rim of the tallest cinder cone. One of them pulls a rope ladder from his knapsack and fastens it to the ground by pounding two steel pegs into the cone with a hammer. Then, one at a time, the men drop into the cone.

Turn to page 65.

"I'll take care of the big guy with the sword," you tell Jon. "As soon as he gets to the top, pull up the ladder. We'll trap the other men down there."

You sneak around to the far side of the rim so that you are behind Boris as he comes out of the cinder cone. Once he has emerged, you give him a hard shove. The thief is taken by surprise, and he tumbles clumsily down the side of the cone, landing with a grunt.

"I did it!" Jon calls to you triumphantly. "I got the ladder up." But you're running after Boris, keeping your eyes on the Silver Sword. Behind you, Jon warns you to be careful. Frantic shouting rises from the large cinder cone, but you're concentrating so hard on the sword that everything else is a blur.

Before you know it, you are grappling with the heavy man, who's at least twice your size. He's lying on his back, struggling to get up. You use all the moves you've learned from wrestling with your brother, and finally, you feel the hilt of the Silver Sword in your hand. With one hard tug you pull it from Boris's belt.

Turn to page 24.

It's difficult to ride through the bamboo quietly. But luckily a breeze comes up, and the knocking of the bamboo muffles the sound of your horses' hoofbeats.

"I see something ahead," Jon says. You approach a clearing where the bamboo has been cut, and the sun is able to reach the floor of the forest. At the edge of the clearing is a bamboo shack.

"Someone must live here!" Jon exclaims. As you ride closer, you hear the voices more clearly. Then you hear a nasty laugh.

Jon is furious. "Camping here is illegal. Maybe the campers are tourists who aren't aware of the restrictions here. We'd better let them know."

"Wait!" you whisper. "I have a better idea. Let's sneak up and try to hear what they're saying."

If you decide to sneak up on the shack, turn to page 50.

If you decide to try to warn the campers, turn to page 75.

Slowly it grows dark, and the moon rises over the Pacific. All is quiet on deck. "There it is!" Jon says suddenly. Approaching the *Molokai* is a dark, sinister-looking ship. But things aren't happening the way the captain said they would. There's been no distress signal, no radio call. Jon dashes below to warn Captain Zardo. As the ship nears and drops anchor, you can make out her name, *Kapu*, which means "forbidden" in Hawaiian. You shud-

der. A dinghy is lowered over the side of the boat, and three men climb in. The motor starts up, and the dinghy moves toward you in the dark water.

Turn to page 72.

You set up camp, muttering, "What a waste. We'll never find the Silver Sword at this rate." Jon remains silent. But you both feel better after a hearty dinner.

Soon it has grown completely dark. The sky is clear and full of stars. You can see the Milky Way and make out lots of constellations.

"It looks like a planetarium!" Jon exclaims as you lie on your backs, gazing up at the stars. Just then a shooting star blazes across the sky. The night birds begin their evening chorus. You hear the sounds of the iiwi, the akialoa, and the owl. Soon you drift off to sleep.

"Wake up, wake up!" You sit up, startled, and glance around. Jon is curled up in his sleeping bag not far away, snoring lightly. "Wake up!" you hear again.

In the highest branch of a mamane tree is an owl.

"Eruption, eruption!" it hoots. "Go home, go home." Then, silence.

"I must have been dreaming," you say to yourself, and go back to sleep.

In the morning you tell Jon about your strange dream. He shivers and says, "That gives me the chills."

"Suppose it was some kind of sign," you say. "Maybe we should head home."

If you decide to ignore the owl, turn to page 57.

If you want to follow the owl's advice, turn to page 106.

"Follow me," you whisper to Jon. As quietly as possible you sneak up the slope of the cinder cone to the rim and peer in. Below the thieves are cramming their knapsacks with small packets wrapped in brown paper.

"Hey, look!" Jon whispers. "Those packets are stuffed with money. I bet they're counterfeit bills!"

But you have your eyes on the largest man. In his hand is a gleaming silver sword.

"When we sell this beauty," he is saying to the other men, "we can retire in style." He slips the sword carefully into his belt. "Okay, finish up and we'll get out of here. Meet me outside in a few minutes."

"That must be Boris, the leader," you say. "And he's climbing up the ladder!"

"What do we do now?" Jon asks. "There are three of them and two of us."

You haven't planned that far ahead, but you have to act fast. "We can pull up the ladder so they're trapped inside," you say.

"It may be too late," Jon says. "Boris is already halfway up."

"Or," you add quickly, "we can tackle the guy with the sword when he comes out."

If you try to trap the thieves inside the cinder cone, turn to page 27.

If you wait for Boris to climb out, turn to page 60.

You turn Makena toward the airport, galloping between the lines of stopped cars that are jamming the road. Within a few minutes you have raced past the gate and are near the runway. You sigh with relief when you spot your parents and brother just climbing into the single-engine Cessna. Your father has already started the motor.

You dismount and throw your arms around Makena's neck, blinking back a few tears, then race onto the runway.

"Thank goodness you're here!" your mother cries, hugging you.

"We waited as long as we could," your father tells you grimly. "We didn't think you'd make it."

"X-Y-one-one-three, cleared for takeoff," comes a voice over the radio. The Cessna taxis down the runway and soars into the sky.

Turn to page 78.

After you tell him you'd love to help out, Captain Zardo explains his plan. "You kids are going to pretend to be deckhands. You'll stay on lookout tonight. Meanwhile, my men will hide below. I know how these guys operate. Some time after dark, they'll send out a distress signal, radio for help, and ask to come on board. How many did you say there were?"

"It sounded like three."

"Okay. You pretend you don't know anything and let them on board. Then we'll surprise them. We'll be ready, and we'll have them surrounded." The captain rubs his hands together. "Finally, my chance to catch those goons. They've been plaguing these islands for too long."

"What do you want to do until it's time to set sail?" Jon asks after you have left the *Molokai*.

"We should do something with the horses," you say. Then you remember a friend from school who lives nearby. "Julie has a horse. I'll bet she'll let us turn the horses out in her corral."

You ride over to Julie's. She agrees to look after Makena and Hana and then offers you a bite to eat.

Later, you walk back to the harbor. At dusk, the *Molokai* leaves the pier. You and Jon position yourselves on deck to wait.

Turn to page 62.

You realize that Jon has disappeared. In a moment he returns with a policeman and the same Coast Guard officer you visited earlier. The three of them stare down at you.

"I want this kid arrested for attempted robbery," the man orders. "The thief tried to steal my boat."

"I was going to return it," you protest, appealing to the Coast Guard officer. "You know those crooks I told you about? Well, one of them got away, and I was trying to catch him. Now he's gone for good." You look out at the ocean, but the dinghy is nowhere in sight.

"I saw him too," Jon says. "He made off in a dinghy. My friend only wanted to stop him. We think he's got some stolen goods."

Turn to page 41.

The lava starts flowing down the mountain so quickly it takes your breath away. You, Jon, and your horses are soon caught in its fiery path and washed out to sea. No one ever finds out what happened to you.

The End

Moments later the three men call up and ask to board your ship. You let them on the *Molokai*, and then things happen quickly. Captain Zardo and his crew of seven rush onto the deck, armed with pistols and knives. Into a megaphone the captain shouts, "You're surrounded. Drop your weapons." You hear more footsteps and then a commotion as another group of men races onto the deck. You count at least ten, maybe more.

"You drop yours," one of them commands. More thieves! Zardo and his men are outnumbered. Their weapons clatter to the floor, one by one.

Then you recognize the voice of Boris, the man you heard in the bamboo forest. "Clever, Captain Zardo, but not clever enough. My men have been hiding in your boiler room. It looks like you're outnumbered. No one will get hurt if you do as I say."

Turn to page 95.

"I'll wait while you collect them," you finally say. "But I won't help you take them."

"You really *are* superstitious, aren't you!" Jon says with a grin. You watch as he chooses half a dozen pieces of lava and puts them into his saddlebag. Then you proceed down the path to the crater bottom.

You feel content and confident that this time, for certain, you'll find the Silver Sword. You hum cheerfully to yourself.

Suddenly, Makena trips and goes down on her knees. You tumble over her shoulder, landing with a crash on the ground.

"Are you okay?" Jon cries, alarmed.

"I'm not sure." You lie still for a moment then tentatively stand and brush yourself off. "I guess so. Nothing's broken. I'm just banged up."

"It's a good thing you didn't go over the side of the trail!"

Turn to page 93.

It's too late to go back into the crater. You'll have to continue your search for the Silver Sword next weekend. A few days later, you receive a phone call from the president of the Maui Wildlife Society. She invites you to a luncheon where the Society will present a medal to commemorate your actions in helping to preserve the nene. You accept with pleasure!

The End

You and Jon get off your horses, and Jon knocks on the door of the bamboo shack. Silence. He knocks again. The door opens an inch, then all the way, and a very large man steps out. Jon's expression changes when he sees how enormous the man is. You can't think of anything to say.

Finally Jon speaks up. "Hi!" he says timidly.

"What do you want?" the man bellows.

"We're . . . lost," Jon replies, struggling for words. "We're, uh, looking for Haleakala." The man starts laughing so loudly that the little shack vibrates. Jon cowers. The man points toward the summit of the mountain. "Up there," he hollers. Then he crams his large body through the small door and slams it shut.

Turn to page 84.

When you arrive at the Bubble Cave, the sun is already high in the sky. You get off your horses, and just as you're about to enter the cave, a bird swoops so low that you and Jon have to duck to avoid its flapping wings. Then it attacks again, practically knocking you off balance.

"That's odd," you say.

"What's odd?" Jon asks.

"That was an owl."

"So what?"

"So owls sleep during the day. I've never seen an owl in flight at this hour . . ." All at once you remember what happened during the night. You and Jon stare at each other. Maybe it wasn't a dream after all! You both shout, "Let's go!" at exactly the same time.

The End

As you head in the direction of the big island, Hawaii, you hear a deafening roar and suddenly the sky grows dark. An ash-laden cloud has engulfed the plane.

Your father maneuvers the aircraft skillfully and soon the cloud is behind you. Over your shoulder you see smoke, fire, and lava pouring out of Haleakala. The lava rolls down the side of the mountain, razing trees and blackening the landscape.

As you approach the runway on the big island twenty minutes later, all you can see of Maui is a cloud of smoke and ash.

The End

After lunch, you stop for a milk shake. When you return to the pier, a large crowd has formed. You and Jon squeeze through the people and see a man in a Coast Guard uniform and three island policemen handcuffing two men. You watch until they are led to a waiting police car that speeds off, siren blaring. The crowd disperses.

"So much for that," Jon says. "Too bad we missed most of the action."

"Wait a minute. We heard *three* voices coming from that shack. Only two men were arrested. That means one of them is around here somewhere, and he's probably got the loot." Then you add, "I wish I knew what the loot was. It could be the Silver Sword."

"Maybe we can find him!" Jon exclaims.

"I bet he'll try to make his escape by sea," you say thoughtfully, glancing at the dock. You race down to it and look around. Sure enough, a rubber dinghy is zipping away at top speed.

"I bet that's him!" you shout. But no one pays attention. You'll have to do something yourself. You look around. The keys are in the ignition of an empty boat right in front of you. You jump in and start the motor. "Come on!" you yell to Jon.

"What are you doing?" Jon screams. "Are you crazy? You can't take someone else's boat!"

You don't have time to argue, but it looks as if Jon needs some persuading.

If you yell at Jon to get in, turn to page 55.

If you decide to go alone, turn to page 85.

"I'm going to the ranger station for help!" you tell Jon as you climb onto your horse. "It's not far from here." Makena takes off at full gallop, kicking up clouds of sand behind her.

When you arrive at the ranger station, you're out of the saddle even before your horse has stopped. You quickly tie her to the hitching post, race to the cabin and knock loudly.

The ranger is eating lunch. She invites you into the cabin. "Someone's fallen into the Bottomless Pit," you say breathlessly. "We'd better hurry. . . . I'm not sure if he's hurt."

Turn to page 94.

To find the *heiau*, you take the trail made by the ancient Hawaiians for traveling across the crater. It's marked by piles of stones called ahu set at intervals in the landscape.

You and Jon descend to the bottom of the crater, carefully following the ahu, and come to a stone road. Supposedly, it was built many years ago by King Ola himself. Makena and Hana trot along. You pass a barren, moonlike landscape of multicolored cinder cones and windswept plateaus of ash and hardened lava.

Now comes the hard part, the climb up the far side, you think when you arrive at the other end of the crater. "Take it slow," you call back to Jon. "It's steep here. And don't stay on my tail, because rocks and pebbles will probably slide down on you."

You begin the climb up the trail. The horses heave and puff as they labor in the deep sand and loose stones. Along the way, you notice that the ground has started to vibrate slightly. Smoke is curling up from the high ridge. With a sinking feeling you realize that this volcanic activity could easily start a landslide.

"Step on it," you yell to Jon, who has fallen behind. But it may be too late. Above you, a large rock has started to slide down the mountain. It gains momentum and collects other rocks and debris as it tumbles down the trail.

"Landslide!" you yell to Jon. "Follow me!"

Turn to page 39.

"It could take days for help to arrive," you tell Jon. "At least if we try to get out now, we'll have our full strength."

"Okay, I suppose it's worth a try," Jon answers.

You and Jon lead the horses along as you try to find a path among the rocks, but Makena and Hana slip and slide helplessly—and it's rapidly growing dark.

"It's useless," Jon says finally. "We'll have to leave the horses behind if we want to continue searching."

"If only there were more light," you say, miserable at the thought of leaving Makena and Hana.

"Hey, what's that?" Jon exclaims suddenly.

You look up. On the very top of the crater wall stands a small dark man silently twirling an enormous lasso.

Turn to page 16.

"I don't trust that guy," you say to Jon once you're a safe distance from the cabin. "I'm going to do some investigating." You tiptoe around to the back of the shack with Jon at your heels. Stacked up against the makeshift building are at least a dozen bamboo cages, each one containing a nene, a breed of Hawaiian goose. Only forty years ago, there were less than fifty nenes in the wild. Since then, they have been rescued from near extinction and are now a protected species. Because they live only on Maui and the big island of Hawaii, they are very rare and very valuable.

You are sure you're about to crack the case of poachers who are catching and selling off the nenes that live inside Haleakala Crater!

Turn to page 56.

There's no time to talk your friend into coming. You slip the powerful engine into high gear, and the motorboat practically flies across the waves toward the high seas.

You scan the open ocean until you spot the dinghy. You realize you are gaining on him quickly. Suddenly you feel nervous. If you catch up with the boat, how are you going to stop it? And what if the man is armed? Maybe you can just get close enough to make out the identification numbers on the boat and the details of the man's face.

With new hope, you race on, the motor deafening you and sea spray drenching your face. You squint, your eyes burning. You can almost make out the writing on the dinghy. You can tell that the man is bald and has a bushy beard.

Turn to page 96.

"Okay, now we have to take a few readings," Dudley says. He shrugs off his pack, digs around in it, and produces a gadget that looks like a tape measure attached to a transistor radio with a tiny video screen.

"Pretty high-tech," you say.

"My vibroelectrosystometer," the archaeologist explains proudly. "State of the art. All we have to do is measure the distance around the rim of the crater and the diameter of the crater, if we can, and this instrument should be able to tell us the depth of the Bottomless Pit, to the millimeter."

"But we already know that," Jon protests, exasperated. "The sign says Bottomless Pit, Thirty-Five Feet."

Dudley ignores him. "Here, you hold this." He hands you the end of the tape measure and starts backing up. "Now, I just bring this part to the edge of the pit and—"

"Look out!" you yell, but it's too late. The archaeologist has toppled over backward into the Bottomless Pit! You hear a muffled crash.

"What'll we do now?" Jon asks.

If you decide to try to rescue Dudley yourself, turn to page 40.

If you decide to get help, turn to page 81.

"Really, sir, it can't hurt to notify the Coast Guard," you persist. "Maybe we can all work together." The captain chews on the end of his pencil thoughtfully. "No," he says finally. "But if you kids want to tell them about this, I can't stop you."

You thank the captain and wish him good luck. A short while later, you're in the Coast Guard office repeating your story to an officer behind a big desk. He asks you for a description of the men inside the shack, but you can't give one. You never had a look at them.

"Maybe you better go undercover," you add after you've finished explaining. "Captain Zardo says we don't want to scare them away. We want to catch them in the act."

The man behind the desk smiles. "Thanks for the advice. I think we can handle this." As you leave, you hear him pick up his phone and say, "Get me the police chief."

"I have an idea," you say to Jon. "Why don't we hang out at the harbor? Maybe we'll see those men get caught. We might even be able to help." You check on your horses, give them some fresh water, and then start wandering around the pier, keeping an eye out for suspicious-looking people and activities.

After a while Jon announces, "This is boring, and I'm starving. I'm going to get a hamburger and some fries."

It's been hours since you've eaten. "I guess I'll come," you say.

Turn to page 79.

Suddenly you remember what you learned in class about King Ola's sword; according to the legend it has the power to cease a volcanic eruption!

You grab the sword from your belt and wave it wildly as you fly down the steep hill alongside the lava flow. Jon and Hana are at your heels. The lava continues to rush toward the village.

"Nothing's happening!" Jon yells.

Desperate, you fling the sword into the liquid fire. It lands point first in the lava. You rein in your horse and hold your breath.

Turn to page 18.

The Lava Tube is so narrow you have to crawl on all fours and sometimes even slide across the rocks on your belly. Something sharp tears your pants. You are completely surrounded by darkness, except for the light from your flashlight. All you can hear is your own breathing.

The flashlight flickers and goes out. Jon grabs your arm. You shake the flashlight. When the light comes on again, it's very dim. "Darn," you cry out. "I can hardly see! I can't figure out what's wrong. I replaced the batteries right before we left." Then you remember. "The river," you say. "It got soaked when we crossed the river this morning."

"Let's turn back, okay?" Jon says, his voice trembling a little.

"We're at least halfway through already. If we keep going, pretty soon we'll see light from the other side," you reply.

The bulb flickers and goes out. You give the flashlight another good shake. This time nothing happens.

If you decide to continue through the Lava Tube, turn to page 7.

If you decide to turn back, turn to page 35.

As you head toward the Bubble Cave the crater looks magnificent in the fading light. Makena and Hana, rested and well-fed, trot on, competently dodging rocks and bushes. A full moon comes up and illuminates the trail.

Finally, you slow the horses to a walk. "How much farther?" Jon asks.

"We're almost there. The cave is a perfect place to camp. We can get up early and look for the sword in the morning."

At last you reach the Bubble Cave. You eat a satisfying meal as you watch the moon sail across the sky and disappear on the other side of Haleakala. You yawn and say, "Time to hit the sack."

You climb into your sleeping bags in a corner of the cave and doze off. Suddenly you're awakened by a pointed shaft of silver light next to you on the ground.

Turn to page 101.

"You're right, I guess. We'll have to wait," you tell Jon.

"I wish there were some other way for us to get out of here," he replies.

Several minutes pass. The only sound is the soft, sad sigh of the nene, the Hawaiian goose that lives inside the crater.

"That's it!" you exclaim.

"What?"

"We could catch a nene and tie a message to its leg. You know, like they do in movies with pigeons."

Jon is unimpressed with your brainstorm.

"It may be our only chance. We've got to give it a try."

Turn to page 108.

Makena has recovered her balance. "It looks like she tripped on a lava rock," you comment, examining the horse for bruises. Dismayed, you see a bent horseshoe a few feet behind you. "And, look, she threw a shoe."

"We can't go on then," Jon says with disappointment. "This is rough footing, and you don't want to lame up your horse."

"So much for finding the Silver Sword today," you say glumly, giving Jon an "I told you so" look. You turn Makena around and head toward home.

Later, when Jon thinks you're not looking, he removes the lava rocks from his saddlebag and carefully sets them on the ground.

The End

You help the ranger saddle her horse, and together you canter back to the pit. Jon is waiting anxiously. "Dudley says he's found the Silver Sword!"

"I did, I did!" you hear Dudley yell from the pit.

With the ranger's help, you hoist the archaeologist out. She examines his find and says, "I'm sorry, Dr. Crake, but this isn't *the* Silver Sword. It bears markings that indicate it's nineteenth century, probably Japanese."

"Oh, well," Dudley replies, starting to add the sword to his pack. "It's better than nothing."

"And it belongs to the state," the ranger goes on. "Any relic found on public land is automatically the property of the government."

"What will you do with it?" Dudley cries.

"It will probably be put in a state vault for the time being," the ranger answers.

"That's even worse than a museum," Jon mutters under his breath.

The poor archaeologist looks defeated.

"Dr. Crake, why don't you come home with me for dinner?" you suggest. "We could both use a break from our search!"

The End

You, Jon and *Molokai's* crew are ordered into the captain's cabin and held at gunpoint while the thieves round up the valuables on the *Molokai*. The cargo is taken by loads in the dinghy to the waiting *Kapu*.

At last Boris reappears. "Okay, you," he says, waving his pistol toward you. "You're coming with us." Then the cold metal weapon is pressed against your temple, and you know better than to argue.

The End

And then your powerful motor sputters and stalls. You turn the ignition key repeatedly. Nothing.

You check the gas gauge. It's empty.

"Darn!" you yell, giving the gas can a hard kick. "Just my luck." You watch the escaping boat get smaller and smaller on the horizon until finally it disappears.

The End

You want to get to the harbor quickly, but you have to ride slowly through the bamboo forest so that you don't make too much noise. Gradually, the bamboo becomes less thick. You emerge into daylight.

"Hang on tight," you say. "We're going to gallop all the way to the harbor." You spur Makena, and off you go, down to the foot of Haleakala and across the valley to the coast. When you arrive, you hitch the tired horses to a post in the parking lot. The harbor is busy, but you have no trouble locating the *Molokai:* She's the largest ship in port. You approach a sailor and ask to talk to the captain.

"He's busy," the sailor answers. "Besides, aren't you a little young to go to sea?"

"I'm not looking for work," you explain. "I have a very important message. It's urgent."

"Okay, but it *better* be important. We don't have time for fooling around. We set out tonight, and there's lots of work to be done. Follow me." You and Jon follow the sailor aboard the *Molokai* to a small room below deck. Inside the captain is talking to his first mate.

"Captain Zardo, these kids have an 'urgent' message."

Turn to page 104.

As you continue looking for a path through the rocks and stones, you realize that it doesn't seem to be getting any darker. Soon you find a way for you and the horses to climb back to the trail above the landslide.

Just as you reach the rim of the crater, the last of the sun's rays dip below the horizon. You turn to look for the small dark man, but he has disappeared.

"It *was* Maui," you tell yourself.

The End

"The Silver Sword!" you exclaim, sitting up.

"Freeze!" yell two voices.

"Wha . . . what!" says Jon sleepily, getting up on an elbow.

Two high-powered flashlights shine in your eyes. The light blinds you. "Who are you? What's going on?" you cry.

"We're rangers," one of the men responds. "Who are you?"

Turn to page 110.

"Something tells me that the Bottomless Pit is the next place to look," you say to Jon.

"All right, it's your search," Jon says, shrugging.

You head along the trail to the Bottomless Pit. A short while later you come upon a funny-looking man carrying an enormous, crammed backpack. He is walking slowly down the trail ahead of you. As the horses approach him, he jumps and turns around. Several pieces of equipment go flying out of his pack and land with a clatter.

"My goodness," the man cries, collecting his possessions. "You startled me!" He looks disoriented.

"Are you lost?" Jon asks.

"Heavens, no. My microentopograph indicates my exact location," he responds, showing you what appears to be a pocket calculator.

"What's all the equipment for?" Jon asks.

The man produces a business card. "Dudley Crake," he announces, as if expecting a response. "Archaeologist."

You and Jon look at him blankly. "You may not have heard of me yet," he explains, "but once I find King Ola's sword, I'll be famous."

"The S-Silver Sword?" you stammer.

"Yes, I need it to complete an exhibit at a major museum in New York. Once I'm finished, they'll name the entire archaeological wing after me. Say, maybe you'd like to come along and help me. My find could prove to be a major contribution to modern archaeology."

Turn to page 38.

The captain eyes you skeptically. Finally, he dismisses the sailor and asks you what you've come to tell him. Quickly you relate everything you heard at the bamboo shack.

"I think we should warn the Coast Guard," you say, when you have finished your story.

"Not yet," Captain Zardo replies. "Those guys see the Coast Guard around here and they'll split. But if we get them on board, we have a chance of catching them red-handed. Will you help me?"

*If you decide to help Captain Zardo,
turn to page 68.*

*If you decide to try to convince the captain to
notify the Coast Guard instead,
turn to page 87.*

"I hate to give up looking for the sword before we've begun, but maybe we should get out of here," you say.

To take your mind off the Silver Sword, you challenge Jon to a race across the field that lies ahead. The horses charge forward, frisky in the cool morning air. Makena wins by three lengths.

It's late afternoon by the time you approach your ranch. Your brother Kevin runs out to greet you before you've even dismounted.

"They've found the Silver Sword!" are the first words of his mouth.

Your heart sinks. You've always been positive you'd be the one to discover it.

Turn to page 111.

You continue the long hike across the crater floor. The sun beats down, and there is no shade for miles. The horses are soaked with sweat and are too hot to go very fast. When the shrub, sand, and rock gradually give way to taller growth and grass at the wetter side of the crater, you stop and let the horses graze.

"I've got to sit down in the shade," Jon says.

"We don't have much time," you remind him. "We can rest for ten minutes, but that's all."

You and Jon sit down under a mamane tree. "It sure feels good under here," he says, stretching out in the shade. You start to feel drowsy. You can barely keep your eyes open. . . .

"Wake up!"

Someone is tugging at your arm. You come to slowly and realize it's Jon. You sit up. "I must have fallen asleep!" you say.

"Me too. And we slept for a long time. The sun's already going down behind the mountain."

You look around with dismay. "Not only that," you add, "but the evening fog is rolling in fast. If we get caught in that, we're not going anywhere."

You sit in silence for a moment.

"What should we do?" Jon asks.

"We can stay right here for the night," you answer, "but if it rains, we'll be soaked. Or, we can try to make it to the Bubble Cave before it gets too dark."

If you stay where you are, turn to page 64.

*If you try to beat the dark and the fog,
turn to page 91.*

108

You dig through your pack until you find your trail mix. You pick out some sunflower seeds, raisins, and peanuts. Then you set them out on a large rock and lie very still.

Hours pass. The sun begins to set. By now there is only a trickle of smoke coming from the crater, so at least you're not too afraid of an eruption. Finally, an unsuspecting nene alights on the rock. Slowly, you creep closer. Then you pounce. But the nene is too quick and takes off.

Turn to page 30.

"We're campers. We're looking for the lost Silver Sword of King Ola," Jon says nervously.

"While there's a volcano alert in effect?" the ranger asks.

"We thought it might be our last chance. If I found the sword, I could even stop the eruption!" you say.

"Well, maybe. But that doesn't mean you can camp illegally," the first ranger replies.

"Illegally?" you ask.

"That's right. You need a permit to camp in the crater, and there's no camping in the Bubble Cave *ever*," the man tells you.

"You never said anything about a permit!" Jon says, looking at you.

"I didn't know we needed one," you answer defensively.

"Well, we won't arrest you this time," says the ranger, "but don't do it again. I want you kids cleared out of here by daybreak. I want you off the mountain entirely."

You nod vigorously and promise to leave. It looks like your search for the sword will have to be cut short.

The End

"You'll never guess where it was!" Kevin continues. "Two tourists from the mainland found it in the Lava Tube late yesterday afternoon. They didn't know what it was and turned it in to the local police. They even got a reward from the Hawaiian Historical Society—five hundred dollars—and their picture was in the paper this morning. I can hardly believe it. After all these years . . ."

You don't want to hear any more. "Don't you have homework to do?" you say irritably to Kevin and head glumly toward the barn.

The End

ABOUT THE AUTHOR

MERYL SIEGMAN attended Middlebury College in Vermont and later earned a degree in law at Villanova University in Pennsylvania. For several years the author practiced law in Vermont. Currently she lives in Lonigo, Italy, where she works in the Italian leather industry.

ABOUT THE ILLUSTRATOR

TED ENIK is a playwright as well as a children's book illustrator. He has illustrated *The Curse of Batterslea Hall, Ghost Hunter, Trumpet of Terror,* and *Statue of Liberty Adventure* in Bantam's Choose Your Own Adventure series and *The Creature from Miller's Pond, Summer Camp, The Mummy's Tomb, Ice Cave,* and *Runaway Spaceship* in the Skylark Choose Your Own Adventure series. Mr. Enik is also the illustrator of Bantam's Sherluck Bones Mystery-Detective books. He currently lives in New York City.

CHOOSE YOUR OWN ADVENTURE

Go On A Super Adventure in a Terrifying New World in the First Choose/Adventure® Superadventure!

January 14, 3000. You've been hibernating in a space capsule for a thousand years. Now you're awake and ready to return to the Earth of the future—but your computer has horrifying news to report. An evil tyrant named Styx Mori has proclaimed himself Supreme Emperor of Earth. He has agents everywhere—even on other planets. And no matter where you land, you face capture—and even death!

This Super Adventure has more—more of everything you like best about Bantam's Choose Your Own Adventure series! It's got more choices, more danger, more adventure— it's the biggest and best CYOA yet!

☐ *JOURNEY TO THE YEAR 3000: CYOA SUPER ADVENTURE #1 26157-6 $2.95 ($3.50 in Canada)*

Buy it at your local bookseller or use this convenient coupon for ordering.

Prices and availability subject to change without notice.

Shop at home
for quality children's books
and save money, too.

Now you can order books for the whole family from Bantam's latest catalog of hundreds of titles including many fine children's books. *And* this special offer gives you an opportunity to purchase a Bantam book for only 50¢. Here's how:

By ordering any five books at the regular price per order, you can also choose any other single book listed (up to a $5.95 value) for just 50¢. Some restrictions do apply, so for further details send for Bantam's catalog of titles today.

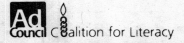